Racecar Driver's Night Before Christmas

Racecar Driver's Night Before Christmas

By Una Belle Townsend

Illustrated by Rick Anderson

PELICAN PUBLISHING COMPANY

GRETNA 2008

The word "Pelican" and the depiction of a pelican are trademarks
of Pelican Publishing Company, Inc., and are registered in the
U.S. Patent and Trademark Office.

Library of Congress Cataloging-in-Publication Data

Townsend, Una Belle.
  Racecar driver's night before Christmas / by Una Belle Townsend ; illustrated by Rick Anderson.
     p. cm.
   ISBN-13: 978-1-58980-565-1 (hardcover : alk. paper) 1. Automobile racing drivers—Juvenile poetry. 2. Christmas—Juvenile poetry. 3. Children's poetry, American. I. Anderson, Rick, 1947- II. Title.
   PS3620.O98R33 2008
   811'.6—dc22
                                        2008004023

Printed in Korea

Published by Pelican Publishing Company, Inc.
1000 Burmaster Street, Gretna, Louisiana 70053

RACECAR DRIVER'S
NIGHT BEFORE CHRISTMAS

It was Christmas Eve morning
'Round the old stock car track,
And the fans were excited
'Cause the drivers were back.

For a couple of months,
No racing they'd done.
They'd missed happy hours
And fun in the sun.

Drivers Junior and Michael,
Who liked to play chase,
Had begged track officials
For a Christmas Eve race.

Named the "Jingle Bell Jammer,"
It soon would begin,
So drivers lined up behind
Pole-sitter McFinn.

Suddenly a strange car
Appeared at the line.
With blinking lights and tinsel,
It smelled of green pine.

Christmas bulbs and bright stars
Were painted on each side.
Out peeked elves and reindeer
A' tryin' to hide.

The old driver's headgear
Concealed part of his face,
And pullin' on gloves, he said,
"May *I* join this race?"

Painted on his helmet,
Each one a neon treat,
Were fudge and fancy bonbons
Looking good enough to eat.

He wore some Christmas decals
On his fireproof red suit.
Mistletoe dangled from
His helmet and boot.

Jingle Bell Jammer

Officials glanced at his car
Then told him he could race,
But bein' a late entry,
He'd start in last place.

Mumblin', "That's all right with me,"
He steered toward the back,
Sang some off-key Christmas carols,
And veered off the track!

When the race got under way
He was far in the rear.
He blasted by three drivers
While sippin' root beer.

Soon he hit a slick spot
Scramblin' around Rudd,
Locked his brakes and hit the wall,
Causing quite a thud.

From under his old car seat—
Knocked loose as he crashed—
Were jingle bells and yo-yos
And peanuts he'd stashed.

At forty laps he pitted,
But drove to the wrong stall.
His crew moved lickety-split
To avoid a nasty brawl.

Tiremen Dale and Adam
Grabbed a tire rollin' astray.
Said Fireball and Davey,
"Whew! No penalty today!"

His team checked for damages,
Then searched for loose wires,
Peeled off a dirty windshield,
And slapped on new tires.

While his racecar guzzled
Gallons of gasoline,
He munched on candy canes,
And one old jelly bean.

Racin' back onto the track,
He clipped Foyt's fender.
Their racecars whirled all around
As if in a blender.

When Bobby broke a drive shaft,
And Greg hit some debris,
The stranger flitted past them
Like a bumblebee.

"Watch that geezer cuttin' in,"
Said Kyle through tight lips.
"Too late," said Matt, swervin' left
And turnin' two full flips.

The stranger yelled, "Don't block me!"
As he sped on by.
"You'll get no Christmas presents,
And no Christmas pie!"

Gordon called, "Move over;
I wanna win this race."
"No way," said the old man,
Sliding into first place.

When he passed the checkered flag,
He was quite a sight.
He started burning donuts,
To his fans' delight.

"Who's the winner?" asked Jarrett,
Starting the applause.
"Well, I'll be," said Jeremy,
"He's old Santy Claus."

When crews walked back to their shops,
They found gifts galore:
Engines, pistons, gears and brakes,
Trannies, valves, and more.

Battery
by
12 drummers
volt Inc

As he left victory lane,
Everyone looked right,
Watched him launch a new race
That would last him all night.

He smiled as he blast past,
And roaring out of sight,
Yelled, "Merry Christmas, race fans.
Y'all have a great night."